Mister Got To Go, Where are you?

Story by
Lois Simmie

Illustrations by
Cynthia Nugent

Red Deer PRESS

Got To Go had the best home

a cat could have at the Sylvia Hotel.

When he was sleepy, he slept on the red striped chairs in the lobby, or on the windowsill in Mister Foster's office.

When he was hungry, he padded downstairs to the kitchen to see what Cook had put in his dish. Got To Go liked a nice bit of fish better than anything. He also liked the tuna sandwiches Miss Pritchett, the desk clerk, gave him from her lunch, and the tasty treats Old Harry, the bellhop, saved from the room service trays.

Life at the Sylvia Hotel was very good.

Every so often Mister Foster,

the hotel manager, said, "My word, is that cat still here? As soon as it stops raining, that cat's got to go."

Got To Go, who had been there nine years, just kept looking out the window at the foolish dogs chasing sticks into the sea.

Mister Foster was very busy managing the hotel. He tried to manage the cooks, although he couldn't cook beans himself. He lifted lids and peered into ovens. "A little more salt?" he would say. After Mister Foster ruined a large pot of Soup of the Day, Cook hid the salt.

In the summer

Got To Go liked to sit on the windowsill outside and watch the people go by. He would cross the street to see the popcorn man and watch the little white things jumping around in his cart. "Has Mister Foster given you a proper name yet?" the popcorn man always asked.

One morning Got To Go saw a truck parked on the street with its back open. He jumped up into the truck and into a pile of leaves. A man came whistling down the street, slammed the back shut, and drove off. When the truck stopped the man opened the back and Got To Go jumped down.

"Whoa! I didn't know I had a hitchhiker,"

the man said. "You'd better go home."
But Got To Go didn't know where home was.
He sat down on the sidewalk to think.

After a while, a man walked by with a parcel that smelled like a nice bit of fish. Got To Go got up and followed the man. He followed him from quiet, shady streets, to busy, hot streets, until they stopped at a quiet place where the grass felt good under his tired paws.

"Where did you find the cat, Jim?"

someone asked.

"He found me," the man called Jim replied. "Here you go, boy," he said, giving Got To Go half his fish and some chips.

Got To Go ate very fast. "You'll eat me out of house and home," Jim said and laughed, since he had neither one. Got To Go rubbed against Jim's arm. "You're welcome," said Jim. "I'm happy to share."

When it started to rain, Jim took Got To Go to a big cardboard box under a bush. "Come on, boy, we can stay dry in here." And Got To Go curled up beside Jim and fell asleep as rain pattered on the cardboard roof.

"Where is Got To Go?"

Miss Pritchett asked Mister Foster. "He wasn't here when I came to work."

"That's odd. He wasn't on my windowsill this morning," said Mister Foster. "Have you seen Got To Go?" he asked Old Harry.

Old Harry asked Cook, who looked at Got To Go's dish. The bedtime snack he had put out for him was still there.

Mister Foster checked in the laundry room. Got To Go wasn't there. He wasn't in the furnace room, or the storage room, or any other room. He wasn't anywhere.

Things did not go well that day.

Miss Pritchett was rude to a guest who kept locking herself out of her room.

Old Harry asked a man if his suitcase was full of rocks.

Cook forgot to put bananas in the banana muffins.

And Mister Foster got a headache and shouted at someone on the phone.

No, it was not a good day at the Sylvia Hotel.

At night in the park, Got To Go dreamed

about soft chairs, warm windowsills, and Mister Foster saying, "Is that cat still here?" When he woke up, he had a strange hollow feeling inside him. On his third day in the park, he rubbed up against Jim's leg and meowed.

"I know, my friend," said Jim, stroking Got To Go. "You're homesick, and that's such a bad feeling. I wish you could stay, but you've got to go." Got To Go's ears pricked up when he heard his name. "Home is where you belong."

Jim led him to the edge of the park and stroked him one last time. "Goodbye, my friend," he said.

Got To Go sat down

on the sidewalk to think. He didn't
know where he was and he couldn't
smell the sea. He saw a man with a
red tinkling cart across the street
and ran over. Cars screeched, horns
blared, and a driver yelled at Got To
Go. But it wasn't the popcorn man.

"Hot dogs," the man called.

Got To Go walked and walked on
the hot, noisy, strange-smelling streets
until the sky turned black and the
rain poured down. Wet and hungry,
he crept into an empty building. He
heard scampering noises overhead
and rustling sounds in the dark and
he shivered through the long night.

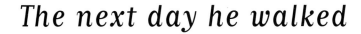

The next day he walked

through forests of legs, and empty streets. A big dog on a leash chased him, yanking its owner off her feet.

Eating some food tossed in a weedy place, he stepped on something sharp that made him limp and leave bloody paw prints on the sidewalk. Sirens wailed, people shouted, sharp noises made him jump, but on he limped, stopping now and then to sniff the air. Still he could not smell the sea.

A large one-eared cat with bare patches of skin followed Got To Go out of an alley. It growled and hissed, swiping at him. Got To Go never had fights. With a shriek, the stray cat leapt, biting and scratching Got To Go ferociously. Round and round they rolled in a tangled ball, pitching into the street where they were almost hit by a bus.

Got To Go crawled up on the roof of an old shed. As the light faded, he licked and licked his sore paw and tried to wash the cut on his head. He felt sick from the fight, and he hurt everywhere. The Sylvia Hotel felt very far away. Exhausted, he fell asleep.

Creak. Creak. Creak. Got To Go woke in the dark to a strange sound. Something was turning around and around on the roof. When Got To Go sat up and sniffed the wind, something wonderful happened. *He could smell the sea.*

There was only one thing

on everyone's mind.

"Where is Got To Go? Where could he be?" And they directed dark looks at Mister Foster.

"Some people could have been nicer to him," said Miss Pritchett.

"That's right," said Old Harry. "Some people could have been a whole lot nicer."

"And now he's gone," said Cook, dangling a big fish he'd been waving around, hoping Got To Go would smell it and come running.

"All right." said Mister Foster, "back to work. We've got a hotel to run."

"A hotel with no cat," Old Harry grumped.

"A hotel without Got To Go is not a proper hotel," wailed Miss Pritchett.

"Thousands of hotels get along perfectly fine without a cat," Mister Foster snapped. He was tired from staying up all night searching for Got To Go.

Got To Go limped along hour after hour,

his bloody paw prints following him. He was so tired all he wanted to do was lie down and sleep, but the familiar smell was growing stronger. He hobbled on as fast as he could. A small dark shadow moving through the windy wet night.

Early in the morning

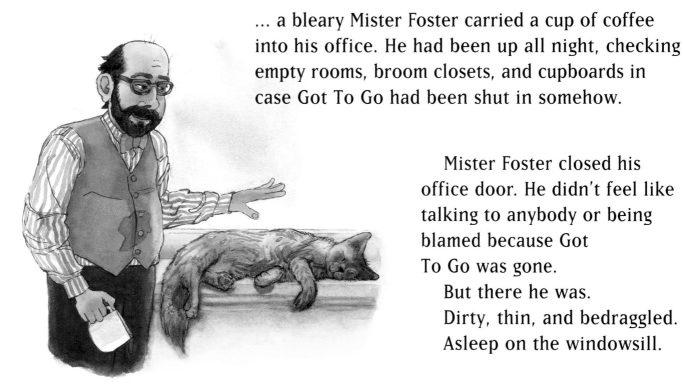

... a bleary Mister Foster carried a cup of coffee into his office. He had been up all night, checking empty rooms, broom closets, and cupboards in case Got To Go had been shut in somehow.

Mister Foster closed his office door. He didn't feel like talking to anybody or being blamed because Got To Go was gone.

But there he was.
Dirty, thin, and bedraggled.
Asleep on the windowsill.

Mister Foster was so surprised that he threw his coffee all over his best hotel manager jacket. He looked at Got To Go for a long while before calling Miss Pritchett.

When Miss Pritchett saw Got To Go, she threw her arms around Mister Foster and ran to tell Old Harry, who dropped a suitcase on a guest's foot and hurried to tell Cook, who dropped the salt in the soup and came running.

They all gathered around and smiled at Got To Go.

And smiled at each other.
And smiled and smiled.

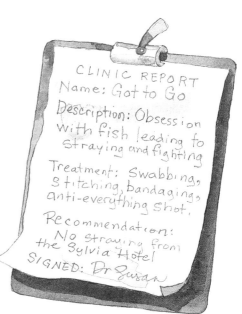

When Got To Go finally woke

and had been given a nice bit of fish, a tuna sandwich, and treats from the room service trays, Mister Foster took him to the cat doctor.

"My goodness, you look like you've been in a war," she said, pulling a large splinter of glass from Got To Go's paw. Got To Go didn't even complain when she stuck him with a needle.

"You should keep him inside," she scolded. Then she handed Mister Foster the bill.
    Mister Foster drove them home in the rain, the windshield wipers whispering, "Got to ... go ... got to ... go," which made them both quite sleepy.

Back on Mister Foster's windowsill,

Got To Go licked and licked his thick gray fur. He licked off the blood, the dirt from the empty building, the burrs from the prickly weeds. He licked away the mean one-eared cat, the big dog, and the empty feeling he had when he was lost. He licked it all away.

He thought about his friend, Jim, and the good people under the trees. He thought about finally seeing the Sylvia Hotel through the rain. He thought about Mister Foster, Miss Pritchett, Cook, and Old Harry.

Then, with a large sigh, he curled up in his favorite place in all the world and he slept.

A few days later,

Mister Foster bustled past Got To Go on his way to the kitchen to manage the cooks. "My word, is that cat still here?" he said. "As soon as it stops raining that cat's got to go."

Got To Go just kept looking out the window at the wet dogs chasing sticks into the sea.

Life at the Sylvia Hotel was good.

It was very, very good.

Published in Canada by Red Deer Press
195 Allstate Parkway, Markham
ON, L3R 4T8
www.reddeerpress.com

Published in the U.S. by Red Deer Press
311 Washington Street, Brighton,
Massachusetts 02135

Edited for the Press by Peter Carver
Cover illustration courtesy of Cynthia Nugent
Cover and text design by Tanya Montini

We acknowledge with thanks the Canada Council for the Arts, and the Ontario Arts Council for their support
of our publishing program. We acknowledge the financial support of the Government of Canada through
the Canada Book Fund (CBF) for our publishing activities.

Library and Archives Canada Cataloguing in Publication
Simmie, Lois, 1932-, author
Mister got to go, where are you? / Lois Simmie ; illustrations
by Cynthia Nugent.
(Mister got to go)
Originally published: Red Deer Press, 2013.
ISBN 978-0-88995-541-7 (paperback)
I. Nugent, Cynthia, 1954-, illustrator II. Title.
PS8587.I314M58 2015   jC813'.54   C2015-904960-1

Publisher Cataloging-in-Publication Data (U.S.)
Simmie, Lois, 1932-
Mister Got To Go, where are you? / story by Lois Simmie ; illustrations by Cynthia Nugent.
[32] pages : color illustrations ; cm. -- (Mister Got To Go)
Summary: "Mr. Fisher, the manager [of the Sylvia Hotel], still talks about how the hotel is no place for a cat but
Got To Go doesn't worry. Then he sees a man carrying a tantalizing parcel that smells like a nice bit of fish
and follows him along the streets for hours until the hotel is nowhere in sight. And nothing is going right at the hotel
with Got To Go missing from his usual windowsill. The staff all come to realize 'a hotel without Got To Go is not
a proper hotel.' Will Got To Go be able to find his way back to his hotel home and family?" — Provided by publisher.
ISBN: 978-0-88995-541-7 (pbk.)
1. Cats — Juvenile fiction. 2. Hotels — Juvenile fiction. 3. Vancouver (B.C.) — Juvenile fiction. I. Nugent, Cynthia II. Title.
[E] dc23 PZ7.S566Mi 2015

Printed and bound in China by Sheck Wah Tong Printing Press Ltd.